MEETING GOD
OR SOMETHING LIKE IT

MEETING GOD
OR SOMETHING LIKE IT

seven short stories

by
Morrie Ruvinsky

First Printing, 2014
Printed in the United States of America
Library of Congress Control Number: 2014942209
ISBN: 978-0-9903098-0-2

Story Thread Press
Santa Monica, California

www.storythreadpress.com

For Alicia

For Jessica and Michael

And for anyone who has ever caught a glimpse of god, and anyone who hasn't

"We must believe in free will – we have no choice."

—*Isaac Bashevis Singer*

"I wouldn't have seen it if I hadn't believed it with my own eyes."

—*Stan VanDerBeek*

STORIES

Meeting God or Something Like It   1

The Lamb   21

A Bedtime Conversation Regarding
Delays in the Second Coming   33

The Crucifixion   39

Podcasting Mercy   57

Kaddish   73

Benny the Healer   85

MEETING GOD OR SOMETHING LIKE IT

You should know going in that when you come face to face with God, chances are it's not going to work out well.

I first met the messiah in an alley, not so long ago. Not between the garbage bins and discarded cartons, as might be implied, but in the light, near the street where the stench includes the familiar aromas of urban life – pretzels, exhaust, unclaimed dog droppings, and various other perfumes not normally associated with the deliverer of mankind – and although I do not, by messiah, necessarily mean Jesus, I can say for sure that it wasn't the glowing guy from the medieval museum collections or the pilgrimage posters.

I'm cutting through the alley because my back is killing me and it'll save a few minutes getting home. I don't know what the rush is because there is nothing there anymore. Some vicodin and heating pads, but they just dull the spasms. They don't touch the real agonies. The unused rooms, the vague lingering scents, the damn hummingbird that still comes to the feeder because I keep filling it.

I'm about to emerge from the alley when everything seizes up, my head, my back, my desire to be alive. I'm in a lot of pain, and I'm scared. I lean against the wall, crouch to be frank, and I'm hunched over breathing real hard when he puts his hand on my head and says that he has come to bless me and I tell him I don't need his god damn blessing and he says it's too late and apparently it was because I could already feel it surge through me and when I looked up to see who he was, he was gone.

It was over in a second. I don't know how I knew – and it was more than just the miracle of my back – but I knew. I had met the messiah. Face to face in a manner of speaking though I hadn't seen enough to pick him out of a line-up.

I told everyone what had happened. That in an instant, my heart had opened. The crippling pain in my mind and in my back simply disappeared. I told the deacon at the first church I passed and he was unimpressed, but I told two priests I saw at Starbucks and they hugged me and said way to go.

I told friends and family, over and over, that I had seen the messiah and they gave me lots of medications and put me in a hospital. A very fancy private place just outside the city so the family wouldn't be quite so embarrassed.

The last thing you expect to happen as a result of meeting the Messiah is to end up drugged and shackled on a suicide watch. Rather, you anticipate that when you open your eyes and see the messiah, you're saved. Period. The world is restored to glory, the Garden of Eden is in full bloom and the meaning of life is not only absolutely clear, but joyful and easy. It's a subtle taste of what it must be like to be a full-fledged Human Being.

You expect a celebration of some kind, some hosannas (not for you, for him), maybe not fireworks but at least a little respect. Anyway, no. I encountered no relief regarding my good news. A touch of skepticism might have been in order, but downright denial? Anger? Accusations? (Pull your fucking act together. Grow up. Did you take your meds?)

In the long run, I came to believe that spending the winter in the hospital probably saved my life. It kept me from wandering out into a blizzard and freezing to death in search of that which everyone assured me was a figment of my imagination. This is only a guess, but all the pressure was probably consuming whatever was left of the blessing. My back was still okay but my head was filling up. I was lost again, shutting down and blowing up all at the same time.

The doctors, it turns out, cannot distinguish between personal agony and crazy. Crazy is easier for them. More comfortable.

They tried their best to comfort me. It was not unusual, they explained, that people experiencing emotional difficulty sometimes have hallucinations. Spiritual experiences, I corrected. Whatever, they agreed, and never once used phrases like psychotic episode in my presence but it was clearly what they meant.

I said yes, yes, you almost got it, pain opens doors, and they said hmmm and I said chances are that even Jesus didn't see God until they actually nailed him to the cross and he realized that yes in fact he was going to die. The Irish doctor said that was a very different matter and the other two decided to up the dosage of whatever the hell they were healing me with at the moment.

By the time the snows melted and it was warm outside again I had learned to deny what I still believed in my heart to be true. You still see the messiah every now and then? Hell no, I laughed, just that one time.

You're sure, just the one time?

I'm sure. God only knows what I was on, I encouraged them, something for the pain I suppose, but I don't need it anymore.

Course once they tag you crazy, crazy is all they see in you. Eventually they came to believe (and convince the family) that I wasn't going to kill myself over having actually touched the tiniest spark of inexpressible divinity (although it is true that I smuggled out over three hundred psycho caps and sleeping pills, enough as the saying goes, for one helluva party.)

The moment they discharged me, I went looking for him. I bear them no mockery. They were kind people, believers, each and every one and it was because they trusted in their own gods that they could be so certain it was my madness and not my witness that they were treating. God bless them, one and all. And if there is no God, let them feel blessed anyway – they work so hard.

I had no idea what this messiah looked like, or even if the form I'd seen was just a transient shape, one meant only for me or only for the moment. God's messenger as shape-shifter seemed not only plausible, but likely. The promise had always been that we would, each of us, see God in our own way. With our own eyes, in our own fashion.

What to do? Where to go? How to look? The answer was as obvious as the question. We are a superstitious lot, and I did what any self-respecting messiah would expect me to, I went back to the place where it happened to recreate the moment that probably never was.

If I went to the wall and crouched, re-played the moment, then I would restore the space in which I had received my blessing and the universe would have no choice but to repair the missing rent. Mend the fabric with messianic presence.

I found the wall, and my place there, and crouched in my best imitation of what I could recall my posture had been. I waited. I shifted my weight a little to the left but it still wasn't working. Probably because I had no pain and couldn't really re-create the hunched over agony that had brought the messiah in the first place. It must have been clear that I was faking, that my crouch was not quite right. Not exactly what it had been or should be.

I adjusted my shoulders a little, and stiffened my back a little less, almost as though I were issuing a challenge. It was answered by one of the city's finest, though of lower rank. A simple patrolman. One must assume that a cop walking the beat is not quite yet the finest but only aspiring to become so.

Sir, are you alright?

I'm fine, I assured him. Just waiting for someone.

Godot? he ventured, assuming that his joke would go over my head because I looked like I belonged in the alley and because I had assumed this posture of pain although no pain was evident in my posture and because he was standing and so the words were in fact over my head.

The Messiah, I answered, thinking go fuck yourself I'm here on a holy mission and truck not with your feeble humor. I thought I had said it only in my head as I had become so used to doing in the hospital, but apparently I spoke out loud. He heard only the messiah portion.

Me too, he said. Nervously. Of course nervously, and he looked around to see if anyone else had heard. This is not the kind of thing you want to be saying if you have dreams of making it to a precinct desk or maybe even a gold shield someday but his courage returned in a moment and he said again, me too.

Here?! In my spot! (That time I did indeed speak in silence.) I was outraged. How awkward it felt to be so possessive. Can one own the messiah, keep him for oneself? But if God could be a jealous god, then why not me, why not this soul in such rutting need of redemption. I didn't go through this winter of hell to share my glimpse of infinite essence with this uniformed shield of commonplace righteousness.

Couple of days ago, he said, that's why I came back.

He'd been chasing a guy – Motherfucker stop or you're dead! – down this very alley when the guy turned around, eyes blazing with fear and bleary from having been chased too many times before, and fired.

It was clear, the cop said, that he had killed me. I watched the bullet, spinning toward my head, it seemed to take forever but it was moving much too fast for me to move when suddenly she was there. She caught the bullet and dropped it at my feet.

She?

I think so. It all happened so quickly.

I was, needless to say to him, very much relieved. At first I thought well good, it wasn't the messiah. Maybe Superman or something, but not my messiah. Not *the* messiah. He was probably hallucinating, he's the one they should have taken to the hospital.

I thought I was hallucinating, he admitted.

Yes.

He handed me the shell. I didn't want to take it. Didn't want to touch it. But he held it out for so long that it would have been extremely rude to continue to refuse, in light of the sanctity of holy moments and all of that. The moment I grasped it, I knew it was real. I could feel her – his – presence immediately. In a fucking bullet!

You know, he said, if you keep crouching there like that you'll ruin your back.

The obvious question for me was why the hell should I believe him. About the bullet, not my back.

He's a cop. He could have found the casing anywhere. At the shooting range. In the precinct lost and found. The fact that he had proof for his story made me all the more suspicious. I had no proof, making what happened to me unassailable, but this bullet – and you will please excuse me for this – shoots holes in his story.

Which would have been the end of that except that he agreed. Artifacts as symbols not only derive their energy from the real thing, but deplete it as well.

It's like, he said, instead of worshipping Jesus, you worship the cross. Or depictions of Jesus on it.

That's why no graven images, I explained.

No weeping shadows on garage doors. No monstrous Buddhas carved into stone cliffs. No Shiva. No Golden Calf, because every symbol carves some piece away from the thing itself. In our case, the bullet made the messiah less potent, not more real.

He said I could keep the flattened shell, as a souvenir and then we both cried out in unison, There he is/There she is – we said at exactly the same time, so precisely synched it was as if we spoke as one. He/She at the same time looking at the same place.

Just exactly what is it that you see, I asked.

You know.

No.

The Messiah.

She?

Look for yourself.

I did and he was no she and I knew for sure then that we were looking at the real thing.

The messiah approached us. He (or she) was waiting for us, and looked nothing like what either of us had remembered. He looked quite ordinary. A disappointment certainly but apparently a necessary one. His full glory would have blinded us I suppose. Or burned us to a cinder. Or turned us to pillars of salt or bunny rabbits humping our way through Arizona.

So ordinary, the messiah explained without saying a word, was what was required.

In fact, for a moment there, it was nothing but uncomfortable silence. It was me who couldn't bear it and I surrendered my pride and my embarrassment and asked directly, are you the messiah?

He just smiled and touched my cheek and the very same power that had surged through my soul the first time did so again.

It is one thing to feel the raging power of total redemption when it flows from something that resembles a wild-eyed prophet from the Old Testament with tangled locks flowing like fire from his skull, but it is very disorienting when it comes from a guy who looks like an Assistant Manager at Costco or a next door neighbor on an afternoon soap.

He touched the cop who fell to his knees laughing more freely than he had since he was a baby and he rolled around on the ground a long time before he regained himself and stood up and nobody passing by even noticed.

What happened the cop asked and the messiah said nothing and the cop said okay and the messiah said go now and be well and he did.

Are we alone now, I asked.

Never.

He began to fade a little, grow somewhat transparent, and I said no, no wait. Wait.

Yes, he said, resuming his presence. What do you want?

I want the truth!

Ah.

I want the truth and all I get is miracles.

The truth? About what?

Christ, I must have muttered.

No, no, he answered, I tried that once, but it didn't work.

He looked at me as if to suggest that if I had a question I should get on with it.

I mistook his attention for impatience, which is of course ridiculous – he would wait forever. Could. My mind raced for what to ask, assuming, incorrectly, that this was my one and only opportunity.

Is true love always true? No, fuck that. Worldly things, stocks or real estate.

No, no. No! As above so below? Will science show us the way? Are there any answers? What is the meaning of life?

I couldn't believe what finally came out of my mouth but before I had a chance to reconsider, I blurted out: Is there a God?

He laughed. What do you care?

Excuse me?

It doesn't matter.

It doesn't matter?

No. You can't understand it.

Try me.

I'm just a tiny fragment and you can't understand me, he said, and when I looked bewildered he said that the combined imaginations of every living soul on the planet was not enough to comprehend the enormity of God whether there was one or not.

Is that a yes or a no?

It doesn't matter.

I don't get it.

I'm the messiah and I don't get it.

I was okay with the God thing. We don't have the brain power to comprehend, okay, fine, makes sense.

Okay.

So forget God, I agreed. But what about you? Why don't you reveal yourself?

I did.

No, I mean really. Let the world see you and be redeemed. Show yourself.

You see me.

I mean to everyone.

I have.

When?

From the beginning.

No.

There is not a living soul, nor was there ever, who has not caught a glimpse of me. Who has not seen at least that. And so many who don't seem to have noticed.

Oh.

You're upset.

No, I lied, tumbling deep into the fathomless pit of despair. He had broken my heart and shattered my soul. I was overcome with insight and shame.

You wanted the truth.

If this was true, that he had always been with us and all we ever had to do was open our eyes, I simply couldn't bear the enormity of our failure. Redemption was at hand from the beginning. All the years, all the generations, all the wars, the cruelties, the inhumanities we have bestowed upon ourselves, it was never necessary?

I said none of it out loud, but he said, yes.

You have always been here, I sobbed. It was an accusation.

Always, he said. Waiting.

We're supposed to prepare the way, not for you, but for us?

I can wait.

What about my wife, my daughters, plucked from me in a tangle of steel and flames. In a fucking instant. Where were you then? Where were you!

Yes, he said. I hear that a lot.

And I got it. It came over me all at once. I didn't think it, I didn't imagine it, I didn't remember it, I just got it. The messiah, by whatever name or notion, had always been with us and all we had to do was open our eyes. And it had nothing to do with God. We had but to open our eyes and in an instant we would be redeemed. Not carted off in raptures and revelations, not restored to our families, but redeemed, here on earth, as though that is what had been intended in the first place.

The messiah smiled.

And I smiled, and began to laugh.

We laughed together and you have no idea what laughter is until you've shared it with the messiah as, it turns out, so many people have and don't remember.

Laughing and laughing, my heart bursting with joy. Long after he was gone I was still rolling on the ground in some sort of cosmic ecstasy and the ambulance came and brought me to the hospital where I was welcomed back with a stomach pump and efficient kindness. They gave me new pills and caused me to be once more shackled and restrained, for my own good.

I laughed, they say, for days without interruption, wracked with joy, afloat with the enormity of our collective promise. And then I crashed, crushed and grieving for the blindness that had driven us to collective despair from the moment we first walked on this planet. I could neither fathom nor escape the depths of this reversal until the messiah came to me for a third and final visit. Disguised this time as a nurse's aid. Young and pretty.

It's you, I said, isn't it?

Yes, she said, it's me.

Will I ever see the light again?

That's up to you, she said. She smiled knowingly, a twinkle in her eyes that I immediately recognized.

And to you, I responded.

She angled the blinds to expose more of the day, then she stroked my cheek and smiled and left.

Truth is, I'll never know if she was the messiah. Or an angel. Or a nurse like she said she was. I couldn't tell anymore.

I was now seeing the spark of divine inspiration in everybody. Every bloodybody.

I had been perfectly content seeing people as an interim evolutionary step. We would pass and something more like *sapiens* would emerge. I was okay with that. I was good with that.

Now I'm fucked. I see transcendent and holy everywhere. In life itself. In every person I pass, in every sentient creature, in every fucking flower. It's too much. It's paralyzing.

I promise you this, next time I see the messiah, I'm going to do something about it.

THE LAMB

In no man's land, between the Israelis and the Palestinians, a young lamb far from his flock found himself trapped out in the open. His right foreleg was broken, jammed into the crevice that had caused it. In extreme pain, he bleated and bawled, calling out in terror for his mother who was with the herd, far away, and could not or would not come.

Three pairs of eyes bore witness. Closest and most focused was a Golden Jackal. In a thicket of underbrush, crouched low to the ground, it trembled with intense anticipation. Drool dripped from the corner of her lips as she stared and twitched her nose at the banquet held fast in the rocks.

The jackal was healthy, but thin, indicating that she had a brood denned somewhere nearby. That her mate was not hunting with her probably meant that he was dead, trampled by encroaching civilization, shot by a settler or a farmer, trashed by an unfamiliar pack.

Whatever the case, she was out hunting on her own and while she might snare a bird or rodent, maybe even a rabbit or two, the trapped lamb was a feast that would feed her family for days, and allow her to rest and recover her own strength.

Barely sixty yards away, her fear of the open space between the thicket and lamb overcame the searing hunger that kept her crouched and poised. She would wait until dark unless something forced her hand.

Abduallah the shepherd was the son of a shepherd, who was himself the son of a shepherd the son of a shepherd the son of a shepherd. They'd lived in these hills since the time of Goliath. Since the time his people crossed the waters from Crete and the heights from Syria. He had just spelled his two sons who had herded the flock through the night.

The stunted hills and rocky scrub on which his sheep nibbled their survival was undergoing revolutionary adaptations. Now the vast rolling desert was becoming civilized. Now his horizon was interrupted by flaring impatient modern developments.

Now, instead of rescuing the lamb, he was forced to sit in the shade of a biblical outcropping and wait. Not at all sure for what. He understood that the new settlers across the valley floor weren't going away. Not any time soon. Certainly not in time for his lamb.

Abduallah's flock wasn't large and every animal was crucial to his family's well-being, but his concern for the isolated lamb was personal, not practical. These sheep depended on him, for food, for guidance, for protection. He felt a father's despair over not being able to rescue his charge.

He didn't blame the Jews. Not all of them, not even all the settlers. Everyone had to live somewhere. He blamed the crazies. The rabid ultra-hostile rabbis and their obsessed minions. The politicians who catered to them. The farmers who turn this beautiful desert to cultivation and un-natural order.

And he blamed his own people too. The terrorists who defiled God and the Koran with murderous and selfish intent. The demagogues who urged them on and the unhappy population who threw rocks to distract themselves from their despair.

How, he wondered, had it become so impossible for the elders to sit together and work out the disputes. Where had all the wisdom gone?

It didn't matter to him whose flag flew where. It didn't really matter by what names this stingy land was called. It had had many. Judea. Philistia. Lower Syria. Israel. Palestine. It only mattered that the people who lived here and shared this place were treated justly.

Allah would be ashamed to know that his children treated their neighbors so badly in His name. He assumed that Yahway would be equally disturbed. Was that it, had God turned away in remorse?

Avrum ben Lazar watched it all from the Israeli side of the valley with standard-issue field glasses that brought everything very close. The terrified lamb. The twitching jackal. And Abduallah, paralyzed by sacred histories on both sides of the line.

Four more months and Avrum was done with the army. Unlike Abduallah, he wasn't born to this land, but like him he was prepared to die for it if he had to. Like Abduallah he was connected to it by myths and mysteries refined and transmitted through countless family tragedies and triumphs. Weddings and funerals, bragging and despair, suckling, holidays, and meals. Food. For celebration, for connection, for survival.

Tidal histories notwithstanding, Avi didn't come to Israel to bully anyone, he came to make peace. And he did. One to one. Person to person. He came to do what the Jews have been required to do from the beginning. Fix the world. Love your neighbor. People are the face of God, and it was his quest to attend to it.

He knew Abduallah couldn't step out into the open valley and not face, at the very least, the fears and angers of the new settlers. It wouldn't take much to get himself shot, not here, this close to the settlement.

For Avi this was less a crisis than an opportunity. He could show the old shepherd the grace that was meant in this place that gave birth to so many Gods and their wandering prophets. He could show Abduallah what was still possible. Dreams of peace were still not yet extinguished.

He had very strict orders not to leave his post and knew that he would face some sort of disciplinary reprimand. A few more months tacked onto his service. Maybe some time behind bars.

Or maybe he would shine a light. Maybe he could make a gesture that would embolden solutions and diminish the power of the mutual terrorism that shackled and demeaned everyone.

So he did. He took the step thinking how ashamed his parents would be learning that he had abandoned his post, how shocked his fiancée's family would be to think she was betrothed to a traitor. The politicians, both right and left, Arab and Jew, would denounce him for taking policy into his own hands. Did he not understand how delicate the situation is?

But as he walked across the valley floor it didn't seem complicated at all. He would do the shepherd a kindness, that's all. If Abduallah in turn did someone else a kindness, good, and if not, so be it.

Avi wasn't looking for a quid pro quo but if there was one maybe the world would be filled with dreams instead of sorrow.

Abduallah didn't know what to make of it, an Israeli heading straight for his lamb. His first thought was that the soldier was going to steal it. His next was to ask God's forgiveness for the suspicions in his heart.

Was this, he wondered, where his sons went wrong? They never thought to ask God's mercy for their hatreds. Unlike him, they grew up occupied, not free.

Abduallah remembers the days when he counted many Jews among his friends. They talked together, smoked together, played together. But not his sons, the only Jews they'd ever known were enemies. Uniformed or not, just enemies. Oppressors. Guards. Others.

Instead they asked God to wipe out the Others. They asked God for the strength and conviction to wage war. They asked God for the courage to live through the indignities, and the fury to grow strong.

As Avi drew closer, he raised his arms and held his rifle high over his head. It was a gesture of peace that he believed the old shepherd would understand. And he did.

Avi had taken a big risk coming out alone this far and now it was Abduallah's turn. He took a moment to pray for some of his sons' courage and then he stepped from the shelter of the boulders and walked out into the rocky flats.

Imitating Avi's gesture of good will, the old man raised his own arms high, holding his staff high in his right hand.

They moved toward the bleating, exhausted lamb.

From two miles away an Israeli patrol – four soldiers in a jeep – spotted Avi in their glasses with his arms raised in what they immediately presumed was a gesture of surrender.

If he were taken prisoner, in this place, in these hills, his family would never see their son alive again. They kicked up a huge trail of desert dust as they raced to the rescue.

Avi and Abduallah were both scared that they may have misjudged the other but they were determined to see it through. They both seemed to understand that this was a moment of something so much more than personal triumph. In this moment they stood outside the damnable atrocities of politics. In this moment they were brothers again, sons of the same God.

Here was how history was made. Here was how the future was formed. Here is how the fertile garden of ethics and morality took shape. Here Yahway walked. Allah. Solomon and Jesus. Here two honorable men could walk in their footsteps.

Each took the other by the forearm and held it in friendship. As equals, not others. In less than fluent Arabic, Avi said he was worried about the lamb.

Abduallah answered in rusty but decent Hebrew, that he was less worried now.

They knelt and calmed the lamb, trying to ease its fears even before its pain. He was truly stuck in the crevice and it would be no easy matter to extricate him. Working together, they might save him.

The sons of Abduallah the son of a shepherd returned with a fresh lunch for their father and when they didn't find him they knew at once where he must be.

They raced to the ledge from which Abduallah had watched the lamb and saw him with the soldier. No, they screamed, No! Father! Father!

They screamed even before they saw the jeep bouncing through the terrible terrain. No! No!

They weren't concerned about the jeep. It would never get there in time. No Father! No!

Abduallah heard something and when he saw the jeep he lost his courage and he ran.

Avi almost had the lamb freed and he wasn't going to give up now. As he lifted the lamb's belly off the rocks, he saw the mine planted beneath it.

The carefully weighted trigger released with a slight pop, and then exploded. It could be heard throughout the valley. It was the sound of dying Gods.

Abduallah was knocked over by the blast but picked himself up and kept running. It was pointless and he knew it. The soldiers cut him down in a rage of bullets.

There was nothing left of the lamb, and only little more of Avi.

With his last breath, Abduallah raised a fist to Heaven and cursed it.

In this land where angels are born, even the jackal ran off in despair.

— ◊ —

A BEDTIME CONVERSATION REGARDING DELAYS IN THE SECOND COMING

I don't think I look anything like you, the Young Man said to God.

–You're a funny guy, God smiled.

–Is that good?

–It's wonderful.

–Thank you.

–But just to be clear, you know that I do, in fact, look like all my children. All my boys. All my girls. My butterflies and my tigers. My kangaroos and my cockroaches. The Bible guys got it wrong. I made everything in my image.

–I know that, but to most people it just doesn't make a whole lot of sense – life is already too confusing.

–It's the teeny tiny little brains. My mistake. People are always accusing me of working in mysterious ways, and I resent that. I'm very organized. Very organized. I mean, look around. No, it's their teeny tiny little brains. I should have made people with much bigger heads and much smaller pricks.

–Like chimpanzees?

–Not everybody knows this, but I was rooting for the chimps. Nothing is written and evolution takes its own course anyway which is probably a good thing because it keeps everything in balance and I like balance.

–But chimpanzees!?

–A little taller maybe. A little less self-satisfied, but I like them. I was hoping they would become the dominant species, but people stood up first. It was the seminal example of evolutionary free will. Because they stood up, they got to use their hands more which made their brains bigger so they got a little smarter a little faster than the chimps – who to this day remain far more content than people, by the way.

–How do you know?

–How do I know! I'm the One who gave them those opposable thumbs, but I don't think their

34

brains ever caught up. First the farming tools, that was hopeful, but then weapons to master each other and enslave each other and now they're trashing the damn place.

–No, you're exaggerating, it didn't happen that fast.

–From my perspective it's been less than an instant to transform the paradise that I created – you do remember the Garden of Eden – into whatever it is now.

–You're disappointed, but there are people trying to make it better. Working very hard. Very generously. There are people who would make you proud.

–I know how much you care about them, you already proved that, but the dilemma can't be solved. Biology outranks ethics. Their bellies pull harder on them than their conscience.

–Is that another one of your mistakes?

–It was one of my dreams, this planet. My jewel. It was special to me. It was the first one, and I made it with my own hands.

–Then why not say yes.

–I know how much it disturbs you. People were a terrific idea, but I think I just overestimated them. So, yes, maybe it was a mistake.

–And all your creatures pay the price.

–And reap the benefits.

–Benefits? Half your world dies of starvation.

–The other half dies too.

–Everything you make dies.

–It's not a mistake.

–Including me?

–My Son.

–No, you can't sidestep this. You have no idea what it was like.

–I have no idea?

–It doesn't have to end the same. I know more now.

–I can't bear to let you go through it again.

–If you won't intervene, somebody has to stand up for them.

–All I said was that Cro-Magnon had their time, the Neanderthals had their time, and maybe now it's time for another evolution.

–They're flawed, not disposable. I'm just asking for another chance. I can do better this time.

–We'll talk about it.

–Thank you.

–It's a shame we can't just play catch, like regular guys. Leave the world to its own devices.

–I dream it sometimes.

–Me too.

–Goodnight.

–Goodnight Son, I love you.

–I know.

THE CRUCIFIXION

The cross was so much heavier than he had expected. Impossible to carry, difficult even just to drag. Especially after the beatings. All night. They kicked, sticked, whipped, pummeled and scourged him. Mostly just for the fun of it.

At first the Man would cry out in pain each time he was struck.

Later he just whimpered in resigned surrender.

The agony lay not in the beatings, but in the certain knowledge that he would die soon but not before they got him up on the hill – they'd never beat him enough to cheat the executioners. That would cost them their wages and probably more.

Some even thought that they were doing him a favor. Crucifixion is a gruesome way to die and the less time on the cross the easier it would be for him. For his family. For those who loved him and hid in the sparse crowd as he lumbered his way to his killing.

It used to be that the Romans only crucified their own – wayward soldiers, Greek slaves, corrupt politicians. Now that the revolution was gaining strength and opposition to the Roman overlords was no longer restricted to the whispered bayous and hills of the outlying territories, a firmer hand was required.

At first the Romans turned to the Jewish hierarchy in search of reliable partners. The Temple priests, and then the rabbis, but neither would or could condone the crucifixions. Execute a Jew! Not only was it against the Law, it was against the very fiber of the people. It was against everything they believed, against everything God had asked of them.

Do justice and love mercy. That was the heart of it. Love your neighbor. And the Romans would ask them to sanction executions? It was simply not possible. Not for the priests, not for the rabbis, not for the seculars, the atheists, the revolutionaries.

On the other hand, it is never difficult for power to seduce accomplices. Some men want too much, and will fawn as much as necessary. They stay close to the powerful, imagining that some of it will accrue to them, but everything turns to dust, even before the body does, before death comes.

The Man hadn't dragged his cross very long before weakness and despair toppled him. The soldiers didn't mind. This job was far less taxing than battles or hunting. Give the Man some drink, a soldier ordered no one in particular.

Two women stepped onto the cobbled pathway. They gave the Man some water and cooled his head dripping fresh rags from a shadowed barrel. They tended some of the more obvious wounds until the soldiers grew bored and one of them poked at the Man with his spear and told him it was time to move on.

It was only then that the Man looked through the hazy glaze of his agonies and recognized one of the women. Her name was Elizabeth. He had known her all his life.

She whispered that she had brought him poison but he refused it. He believed what he believed. He was prepared to die an honorable death for truth and righteousness, not slink away in the comfort of a dream.

It had not been easy, these years. Sometimes he grew discouraged out in the squares seeking converts. More often he was on the run, just steps ahead of the authorities. Well they had him now. His body and his freedom, but not his pride. Not his honor. Not his absolute faith. That, he would reserve and protect until his very last breath.

Elizabeth was not surprised. She knew him well enough and whispered that it didn't matter what they called him, how much insult they inflicted or how much pain he had to endure, the people understood the truth.

The people knew what he was fighting for. The people would not forget.

He managed a few more strides bearing his cross. Every muscle in his body enraged with protest, and he knew that it was nothing compared to what waited for him on Golgotha. He couldn't move and felt the sudden sting of leather strips across his thighs and cried out Oh God help me.

He had given so much and was now prepared in his heart to surrender it all, for God, for his people, for Abraham and Moses and David. But he couldn't move. He felt the lash again but this time said nothing.

He looked to those lining the street. Many had come, not throngs, but enough to escort him with their silent prayers. Another Jew was being led to martyrdom, and they prayed for him.

It was too dangerous to speak out, too dangerous to bless him out loud, so they stood in silence offering their limited courage and their boundless aspiration that one day the Temple would be restored to righteousness and they celebrate all that he had done, all that he and his brave brothers had sacrificed. There they will remember what was thrust upon them in these horrible days.

It took a very brave soul to step from the crowd and offer to help. A boy really, but large and strong already, and he stood with the Man and took the weight of the cross on his own shoulders. He thought the soldiers would probably beat him, but he knew in his heart it was the right thing to do.

Love your neighbor. Do justly and love mercy. He'd heard it all his life.

But the soldiers couldn't have cared less. As long as the cross kept moving, they were content inching along. No one's in a hurry to get to the hill.

The young Mordecai would be celebrated by all Jerusalem for his courage, by everyone but his mother who railed at him for weeks afterward about the unnecessary danger he volunteered for, but it was bigger than that. His younger cousin, inspired by the display of decency, fled the protections of the shielded doorways and ran to help. He took a place a few feet behind Mordecai and the Man, and noticeably lightened the burden.

From there the miracle began. Men, strong and weak, scholars and tradesman, farmers and a priest, stepped to the street and took up positions under the three hundred pound cross and the Man himself was transported into what almost amounted to a reverie. The gallows wood became light as a feather as the community gathered in the light of God.

One of the men, not even the rabbi, shouted out we have a minyan! And all at once they began to pray. All at once. No priest required, no announcement to start, just ten men together uttering the holiest of their prayers. Singing together. Not a dirge, not a plea, but a simple chant of joy. *Shema Yisroel Adonai Elohaynu, Adonai echad. Hear O Israel, the Lord our God is One.* The universe is whole.

From the sidewalks and the windows the song was joined and carried along. The Man sang with them, God is One. It is the last sound that every Jew hopes to hear, the last sound they hope to have on their lips when they die. Hear me affirm that God is whole, that God makes all the fragments of the universe a unity. It's the sound that says no more multiplicity of godlets – one for rain, another for potatoes, another for love, another for fields and gardens. Godlets for every purpose, joined by this one song that reminds the world that there is only One, by whatever names it is called, but only one God, one universe that includes us all in some divine arrangement no one will ever understand.

But they will sing. All along the way to the hill and the soldiers didn't care. It was certainly unusual but pleasant enough and by the time they reached the hill and lay the cross down for the crucifixion, the Man himself had been transported. Freed. Personally redeemed.

He had a glimpse of God, in the people who defied their conquerors and prayed with unfathomable joy. They couldn't stop the crucifixion, but they could bring God to it. They could bring God close enough to whisper in the Man's ear – Here Am I.

Even as they stripped the Man naked and tied him to the cross, he continued to whisper the words and to know he was going home. All his troubles were over. He had done well he knew, or God would not be here with him. *Shema Yisroel Adonai Eloheyno Adonai echad.*

Even as he lay on his cross waiting to be hoisted skyward to be seen for miles around in all his humiliating, soiled nakedness, he felt a calm he had never experienced before.

Over and over, at peace with himself even in his agonies, he recited the *Shema.* He knew he had lived his life well. He had loved intensely and completely.

He had honored not only family, but his neighbors and the strangers who came to him for shelter or simple directions. He had fought with all his heart to throw off the yoke of Roman oppression and return Israel to its people.

Despite the daily falls from Grace, he had given everything to try to restore a world where everyone automatically loved their neighbor, where everyone automatically sought out the common good, where Justice and Mercy ultimately restored the joyous simplicity and health of Eden from one end of the globe to another.

Still reciting the *shema* he begged forgiveness for the men he had killed. The magistrates and Romans and soldiers who died because of him. Those yet to die because of him. He believed, hoped, that his death would cleanse the world of his many sins and immediately become a better place. It would give his life both sanctity and noble sacrifice if his dying made anything at all better for those he left behind.

Shema, he said, *Shema, Shema. Shema.*

And then he screamed in terrible agony. He screamed so loud it was heard all the way down at the gates. It was a bellow beyond human comprehension and he hollered out again as they continued to drive the ragged spike through his right wrist, impaling his arm to the crossbeam.

Eventually, he managed to slow his breathing and convince himself that it was done, that nothing would ever again approach the agony he had just experienced. He had made the sacrifice, suffered the worst pain a man could know, and wasn't even aware of tears flowing from his eyes.

The next spike, on his left arm, was far worse. It went through the wrist and also fractured an arm bone, the horrible searing fire would not abate until he was dead.

Every breath, every twitch, even the slightest shift of his hand was like angry armies of fire ants crawling inside his limb from the tips of his fingers up to his shoulder.

He soiled himself again, instantly drawing hordes of hungry insects to the feast. His manhood shriveled, trying desperately to retreat back into his body.

Crucifixion is a cruel and brutal invention, designed to prolong the agony, and enhance the humiliation and suffering. It was intended to punish with ultimate severity. It was always public so that it might serve as an example of the fruits of defiance. Family and friends were always invited, lest they forget.

But like the tortures before it and the ones that might follow, crucifixion has no permanent power. Eventually the administrators of all the abominations are defeated, dismantled, and driven to hells inspired by their own designs. Eventually the Romans will be driven from this land, and eventually the Temple will become holy again.

They drove a larger spike through his feet. He called out to God. Have You forgotten me, he pleaded. Did I not do my best?

There was no answer.

Save me, I can't bear this anymore.

There was no answer. Except this, a moan of deathly relief off to his left. A thief who had been crucified in the very early morning was finally spared further punishment when a Centurion came by on his horse and plunged his sword into the Man's belly and killed him at last.

The Man cried out to the Centurion, come to me, come to me, but the Roman rode on as though nothing unusual had happened. A little local mercy dispensed, nothing more.

In his final agonies, it was not the spikes or broken bones that did him the most damage; it was the certainty of his death. It was the fear. The terrifying unabated fear that nothing, nothing could soothe. He was, he knew, already dead. Even if they released him from the cross and wrapped his bones and staunched the bleeding and healed his wounds and soothed his pain, he would be dead by night. There was the agony.

He was a screaming dead man, voiding any honor he may have earned in his lifetime. Obliterating every sacrifice, every triumph. He could see friends turn away in shame. Family, hiding in fear lest they too be taken.

And though God had abandoned him, he shouted I have not abandoned You.

His eyesight was beginning to fail but not so much that he couldn't see the next execution coming up the hill and the people along the way sang for the new sacrificial lamb but the soldiers were weary of hearing it. They whipped him, and poked him, and he too had the help of others bearing the cross to the hilltop.

The Man saw it was a rabbi. He looked so thin and frail when he finally set his burden down and they stripped him and tied him to his cross. The Man recognized him. It was Yeshua from Nazareth, Jesus to the Romans.

The Man knew of him but had never liked him. The Man had risked his life, had been forced from his family by the circumstance of revolution, and had lived by his wits and his courage, his skills in tactics and battle, and the support of others who also wanted the Romans gone but, for whatever variety of explanations, could not or did not join the battle. It was a very popular, but very spare revolution.

The Rabbi Yeshua, on the other hand, preached. Like the Man, he believed the heart of the Jewish impulse – love your neighbor. Like the Man, he believed that one must love justice and do mercy, and walk humbly with God. But apparently neither a freedom fighter nor a freedom preacher can move the enormous secular power of the Roman military.

While both sought to redeem the people from the yoke of the oppressors, the Man would redeem them now, in this world. The rabbi would redeem them later, in some other world to come. But whether you battle the Romans with your swords, or with your words, you end up here on Golgotha. Calvary the Romans called it.

Yeshua screamed just like the Man when the first spike shattered his wrist. He cried out in agony continuously until his cross was planted upright and he was no longer being actively molested.

The Man thought that if Yeshua's people had joined them in the struggle, the Romans would be gone by now and neither of them would be dying on the cross.

With every weakened fiber of his dying being failing him, the Man turned to Yeshua. Rabbi, he called to him.

Yeshua, with great pain and effort turned to The Man.

Why you, the Man asked.

Yeshua was no revolutionary, no insurgent, certainly no murderer or thief. It seemed unjust, a holy man dispatched like this. Why you, the Man asked again.

I have come to redeem the world, the Rabbi explained.

No need, the Man answered as graciously as he could manage under the circumstances.

I have come to die for your sins, Yeshua explained.

If that's true, Rabbi, the Man demanded, then what am I dying for?

For mine, Yeshua answered. For mine.

The Man began to laugh, Yeshua too, but the pain was too much and they both stopped.

Failing rapidly, the Man could barely see through his dimming eyes, but he could see the Roman coming his way, drawing his sword.

I am done, he told the rabbi.

Drawing what he knew were his last breaths, he prepared to recite the *Shema.* All his life the Man had prayed that when he died, he would die with the mantra on his lips. *God is One. Shema yisroel* he cried out.

No, wait, the rabbi called, your blessing, I beg of you.

The Man stopped short.

I beg of you the rabbi repeated.

With nothing much but their agonies in common, it was clear to the Man that the rabbi had more need of him than God did and he turned to Yeshua.

May God bless you and keep you, the Man offered as the soldier rammed a sword into his belly.

The Man screamed. Yeshua too.

May He make His light to shine upon you...

The soldier sliced the Man through his side and they both screamed again.

And grant you peace.

The Man bled out quickly, but not before Yeshua began to recite *Shema yisroel...*

The Man heard him and smiled, and Yeshua wept.

PODCASTING MERCY

Just yes or no?

–I can't answer yes or no.

–It's a simple question. Is God bigger than the whole Universe? From your ethics class.

–Please don't kill me.

–Answer the question. Does He play by the rules or not, that's all I'm asking.

–God is greater than everything.

–So that's where you got it in your head that you were what, entitled? Because what, God said so?

–I didn't do anything.

–To me, God's smaller than the universe. Way smaller. Not like planet smaller, like ant balls small. For which, mother-fucker, I got you to thank.

–Could you loosen the rope? It hurts.

–Damn you look scared. It's different on that end of the stick, isn't it?

–I'll do whatever you say.

Podcasting Mercy

–That's the spirit, but we're already doing it. We're going public as we speak. The Bluetooth I taped to your ear? We're live, and the podcast'll stay on the cloud forever, for anyone who wants to listen. Today. Tomorrow. A hundred years from now. You're on the record for good, Sweetheart.

–I have nothing to hide.

–Aw c'mon, I give you a shot to come clean and the first thing you do is try to cover your wrinkled ass?

–I never meant any harm. In my heart—

–Your heart? That's what makes you evil. You made us feel special, so at first I thought it was cool. The attention, it makes your head spin, makes you feel like you've been anointed. Chosen, you know? You don't think of yourself as prey until much later, Sweetheart.

–Stop calling me that.

–That's what you called us. All of us. Sweetheart, so you didn't have to learn our fucking names.

–That's not true.

58

–Then say them! Say their names and save them!

–I don't know what you're talking about.

–Put someone else ahead of yourself for once in your life. Show your compassion instead of your cock.

–Please take the blindfold off.

–No. I came to put a stop to you. So maybe my nightmares will go away. And maybe I'll be a better father, and a better husband. And maybe I won't be so...broken.

–Oh my God, you are going to kill me!

–These things are so unpredictable.

–No. We can talk! Why are you doing this!

–To stop the raging in my heart. After all these years. To save myself. And maybe a few others.

–I loved you.

–All of us?

–Yes. I felt—

–We felt humiliated. It was not like the other kids didn't know what was going on. Stop crying.

–Please don't hurt me.

–Hurt you?

–Kill me. Please don't kill me.

–Are you scared?

–I pray for forgiveness every day.

–To who?

–To God.

–See, that right there could be the problem for you, given the circumstances. Maybe that's where it all went wrong for you, you figured God would take all the blame for you, forgive you every Sunday.

–Please—

–Hey, you got Jesus in your heart, nothing can hurt you, right? Didn't you teach us that?

–Yes.

–So, you got Jesus in your heart?

–I don't want to die.

–Yeah, nobody does. Some people have it coming to them though.

–No, no I never hurt anybody.

–What fucking planet do you come from!

–Oh Dear God!

–What about Jimmy Hudson for starters.

–Who?

–He was here six, seven years ago.

–I don't—

–I wouldn't have had the courage to come here if it wasn't for Jimmy Hudson, what happened to him.

–I thought everybody liked me.

–Mostly we were all just scared. We didn't know what was happening to us.

–I was—

–Pray now.

–What?

–Pray.

–No. Oh God. Don't do this.

–I remember saying that to you.

–Thou shalt not kill! Thou shalt not kill!

–You're going to quote the bible to me? You?

–Mercy is God's greatest gift.

–God's what gave you permission to do what you did to us.

–No, that's—ow! You cut me!

–I'm just scaring you.

–Yes. Is the blindfold still necessary?

–The terror you're feeling? It's what I felt every time you came after me. It's good that you know what it feels like.

–What?! What are you going to do!

–Now look, you wet your pants. I guess a little humiliation is good for the soul but too much, not so good.

–Please, I'll do anything—

–Tell the truth?

–What?

–You're not familiar with the concept? Apologize. Make a public confession. Show the world that we aren't the liars. We aren't complicit. We were kids!

–Ooow! Holy Mother—

–Sorry. Slipped. Just a slight nick. Nothing to worry about.

–What do you want me to say?

–What do you want to say?

–I want to apologize, right? From the bottom of my heart to the boys whose trust I abused.

–That sucked.

–I can do better.

–Confession comes with consequences. You know that, right?

–What's that!? What are you doing!?

–Calm down. I'm adjusting the bluetooth. You'll sound clearer. Jesus Christ, you smell.

–Okay! Okay! So...um...Jimmy Hudson...I want to apologize for—

–No, Jimmy comes later.

–Johnny Richmond, right?

–Sure, but he said it was no big deal and he didn't want to have anything to do with this. He said he was so horny back then he would have fucked a duck.

–I meant Johnny *Freeman*.

–He's a druggie in Thailand now. He tutors young boys for drug money and buggers their fathers for the big bucks. He emailed.

–Oh God.

–Screw God. Ask Johnny.

–Okay yes. Yes. Johnny Freeman, I beg your forgiveness.

–How many, Sweetheart? All together, how many boys?

–I don't know.

–How many!

–I don't know!

–Forty-two.

–No.

–I have a letter with forty-two signatures including mine. Forty-two of us whose lives were crippled by you. Forty-two of us who are still so ashamed we all had to think about whether or not to sign on and go public.

–Forty-two boys! That's impossible.

–And we all think that's a small portion. So name us. Apologize to us. Ask for our forgiveness. Say our names and set us free.

–And what do I get?

–What do you get!

–You're asking me to give up everything. For what? For nothing in return.

–You may be the worst fucking human being I have ever known. I ask you to search your heart for a little compassion, and you come up with what do I get!

–No.

–I know so many people who would be delighted to mourn your passing.

–Jack Abruzzi.

–What?

–You think I'm so callous I don't even know your names!

–Yes.

–Jack Abruzzi.

–Don't sound so fucking eager.

–I want to apologize with all my heart to Jack Abruzzi, who I...befriended...when his family moved here from Michigan.

–He's in a coma. Five, six years now.

–No.

–Drunk every waking hour before that. Lived in a fog and finally drove himself into a real brick wall.

–Oh sweet Jesus come to me in the hour of my martyrdom.

–Your martyrdom? Are you shitting me!

–It's not like it was all my fault.

–You're blaming us? Us!

–No, it's the blindfold. It's making me nervous.

–It's not the blindfold you have to worry about.

–I'm afraid of the dark, alright! Why are you doing this to me?

–If you mean why now, it's because tonight Jimmy Hudson hanged himself.

–Do I know—

–In the annex, where you used to take him every Tuesday and Thursday. You can't even remember who he is but the note he left is pretty much all about you.

–Of course I remember him.

–No you don't.

–Why are you doing this to—

–No more Jimmy Hudsons. You're never going to hurt another kid.

–It's not my fault that he—!

–It's all your fault. I was in favor of scorching your balls with a glowing poker every day for the rest of your life, but I was out-voted. Though not by much.

–Wait! Where you going? Don't leave me alone. Please if I have ever done the slightest good in your life, lightened the slightest burden, maybe even lifted a broken heart, doesn't that count for something?

–Redemption? You want redemption. I can't help you with that, that's in your hands.

–You got nothing? Not even the smallest spark I can show God and say see, there was a moment I was a decent human being, so I'm worth saving.

–Because everyone is worth saving?

–Yes. Yes!

–Go fuck yourself.

–Don't go! Don't leave me alone.

–You won't be alone, I'm leaving the phone. It's got a couple of hours left on it. You're going to be a celebrity. Everybody's going to be wanting to talk to you. The cops for sure.

–Not a word. Not another word from me. I want my lawyer.

–Lawyer can't save your soul.

–Not another word.

–It's your soul, do what you want with it.

–Maybe it's too late for me, but why are you making it too late for you? You think what you're doing here makes you a fucking saint?

–No, but I'll pray for you.

–Compassion comes before prayer.

–You're asking me to save the sinner?

–Yes! Help me.

–I got twenty years of rage in me, Sweetheart, and I wouldn't lift you up if your balls were stuck in a gopher hole.

–I need someone to say, yes, I was there when he saw the light and repented. Be a witness. Let your hatred go for a minute and save my soul. Maybe yours too while you're at it.

–Don't push me.

–I'm not pushing, I'm begging.

–You don't deserve any fucking favors, but I do, we do. We all deserve to be free of you.

–Is that yes?

–Okay. Shit.

–Thank you, Sweet Jesus, thank you.

–Sweet Jesus thank you?

–No, you. Thank you. Right?

–I was just fucking with you.

–My very first was Robert Alton. Bobby. I struggled a long time before I gave in to this, I don't know...longing. I hated myself so most of it was sort of innocent, but not all of it. And then Theodore Billets, and I hardly struggled with my conscience at all. And...and...I'm very nervous. I'm not very good with names. I just want to do the right thing....

–Shermy Wallis.

–Shermy Wallis. Yes. Sweet, sweet boy. I remember sometimes we'd go to the gardens—

–Let's stay on track here.

–Shermy, if I have hurt you, caused you any pain, or confusion, I beg you to forgive me.

–Good.

–Harry Lake? Joey Berman.

–My brother.

–What?

–Joey. My brother.

–Oh God, you're Big Junior!

–Nobody calls me that since high school.

–Holy Christ. I thought you were in prison for life!

–Life changes.

–Oh no, Junior, please. I'm sorry about what happened.

–You never came to court when they accused me of cutting up that kid from Arizona. You knew it couldn't have been me, because you knew where I was when it happened. You knew exactly where the fuck I was, you sniveling god-fucking—

–Junior—

–Weeping!? No fucking weeping. I never got to, you don't get to.

–I am truly sorry.

–In your heart? In your miserable heart.

–In my frightened, lecherous, quaking heart.

–I came to get rid of you.

–No. No no no no. Please—

–So I accept your apology.

–What?

–I forgive you.

–If this is a trick—

–I forgive you. I forgive you. For my own sake, I forgive you.

–Oh God.

–You and me, we saved a lot of kids tonight.

–Wait! Where you going? No wait. They can't find me like this!

–Staff'll be here in the morning. Cops too, I figure they'll want pictures before they untie you.

–Not like this! Don't go! Hello?...Are you there?...Junior?...Hello? What should I do? Is anybody listening?...There's Harley's brother Wayne. And the sister once. Just once. And Timmy Costello....Should I just go on? Hello?... Anybody?

KADDISH

The curtains were drawn because the light hurt his eyes, and the room wasn't so much musty as it was medicinal.

They had moved his bed into the living room because the bedroom had become too close even when he was in it alone.

The lingering scent of terminal aging had saturated the walls with its biological indignities and now that the family had gathered, it was impossible.

The living room was the only area large enough to keep the rank perfume of inevitability from choking everyone.

The old man didn't mind the idea, at first. He'd spent many good years in this room, but it was transformed now, alien because he was dying here not living here.

The bed was where the sofa used to be and the sofa now blocked his view of the fireplace. The big armchair where he used to read the paper had been dragged from the window to the foot of the bed and the little stand with the books he was reading was gone. He was too weak to hold a book anymore and someone, meaning well, took the stand out into the hall thinking that he'd be less disturbed if he wasn't constantly reminded.

The opposite was of course true. He missed seeing his books. He missed being reminded about how much more there was to discover, how much more there was to learn. He missed the reminders of all the places and ideas he had visited in the pages of his books, and all those he had once meant to get to. He surrendered those ambitions days ago.

Of all that he had come to know in his eighty-seven years, the only certainty that remained was that if he fell asleep, he'd never wake again. He marveled at how much more practical truth becomes when you have vital need of it. For two days and nights now he had marshaled all his resources to fight the impulse to close his eyes.

He was in terrible pain but he refused his morphine because it made him tired. The drugs took the edges off the pain and seduced him with a thick and warm easiness that almost tricked him into wanting to sleep. But he knew he couldn't close his eyes, even for a moment.

Everyone tried to be helpful, tried to put his comfort ahead of their own terrible sense of impending loss. "Rest, Poppa," one or another would say and then rush out of the room to cry or try not to. The old man could hear them out there. He wanted to comfort them, to hold them like he had when they were children and tell them everything would be alright but they all knew it wouldn't be. Not ever again.

"The curtains," he said with the weakest wave of his hand, barely lifting it from his chest.

"It hurts your eyes, Pa."

"They already hurt."

Someone opened the curtains expecting the light to explode into the room like some ferocious ogre but it was already evening and it filtered in slowly, soothing and luxurious.

"Are you alright, Pa?" someone checked.

"I'm dying," the old man answered.

"Don't talk like that."

"I'm dying," he repeated. Pissed off. It was his dying and he was the one who should be afraid, but it was them. Grown sons, with grown children of their own, and they were the ones who were scared. It was for them he wouldn't close his eyes. They were the ones who weren't ready.

It brought him no measure of peace to know that. In fact, what scared him most about his dying was that he had not taught them how to let him go. He wondered if he could teach them now, but there wasn't any time left.

He only had a few hours at best and his mind was already clouded and adjourning, so how, he wondered, could he possibly convey anything at all that would make a difference?

He had never been a religious man so he had never taught them much about religion. Little more than the basics. Seders for pesach. Sometimes visits to hear the sounding of the shofar on Yom Kippur on those years when mood drew him to it.

There were bible stories, many told in that old stuffed chair that now scuffed the floor at the end of his bed.

In the beginning God created heaven and earth. Or Moses was a little baby floating among the bullrushes or destroying armies of great warriors. Joseph and the coat of many colors. Daniel in the lions' den.

"Daniel in the lions' den," he said. They could barely hear him.

"What, Poppa?"

The two sons in the room with him drew closer. "What did you say?"

"In the lions' den," he repeated knowing full well they would misunderstand.

"No, no, it's alright, we're here."

He hadn't taught them much about religion because without death, there's little need for God. It's helpful to have an authority for ethics and laws and morals, but it's not necessary. Careful attention and genuine compassion lead to the same place. Or purpose, certainly one can find purpose without recourse or reference to religious doctrine.

But death, there is no reasoning one's way out of that. There's acceptance or denial, raging or embracing, calm or terror, but no escaping it without God.

It was easy now for the old man to see that it was death that invented God, made God an answer to the fear. Created God perhaps. Whether real or imagined it was a good answer to the vast incomprehensible universe of which we were not the center.

A single tear rolled down the old man's cheek and his middle son thought it was his death tear, but it was not. It was a tear of sadness as he finally accepted how much he had left, now permanently, untaught. He'd given them poems and science, philosophy and common sense. Baseball. He taught them about love and loving. About accepting it and celebrating it, and now with his life counting down in minutes it seemed like he was prepared to part with anything but the parenting. He was deeply saddened by all that he had never said and by the pressure he now felt to say it before it was too late.

Where was the peace that living honorably was supposed to convey in the end?

His youngest grandson arrived before it was entirely too late. He was more perfect with the boy than he had ever been with any other human being and he was happy to see him. Not happy considering the circumstances, just genuinely happy to see him. The boy ran in and climbed into the bed before anyone could stop him.

"No no no," someone said reaching in vain to grab him. Hard to know who he was protecting.

"Oy, no," someone else echoed.

He lay his head on his grandfather's chest for a long time without saying anything. The old man caressed his forehead.

"Are you dying Zaida?"

"Yes." He never lied to the boy.

"Pa, please, he's just a boy."

"He's a boy," the old man rasped, "and you, you're a child."

"Today, Zaida? Are you going to do it today?"

"Maybe," the old man said, stroking the boy's forehead, "yes, it could be today."

The boy wept. His shoulders shook and he cried and he held onto his frail old grandfather and the old man was immensely grateful that someone in the room had the courage to mourn in front of him.

"I'll never forget you," the old man whispered.

The boy smiled, he always got the old man's jokes.

"Me too, Zaida."

"I know," the old man assured him and then suddenly remembered how he knew and what it was he had to do. When his own father died, also mourning what he had left untaught, he prayed the Mourner's Kaddish for him. And every year after that on the anniversary of his death, and any day in between when he needed to touch him.

Yis-kadal v' yis-kadash sh'mai rabo. The first line, which translates loosely as Yay God (Magnified and sanctified be the great name of God, etc.).

On its surface the prayer is intended to set free and protect the souls of the dead. But really, it is a chant, a magical liturgy to safeguard the spirits of those left behind.

So it wasn't God he wanted for his sons.

And if Truth be told, the old man had no issues with God. (You leave God alone, God leaves you alone.) If his last breath was his last breath and there was nothing else, he was okay with that. He'd had a full life, pain and terror and failure certainly, but love, brimming, and laughter, lots of laughter. Even now he could make the boy laugh.

So it wasn't God he wanted for his sons. And it wasn't religion because he thought that most of it was just ancestor worship in disguise. It was the chant of magic that would heal them and make them men, let them grow when he was gone. It was the magical words bursting with meaning precisely because they were devoid of definition. His sons would never need to know what the words meant, only the sounds. Only the song.

"Yis-kadal v' yis-kadash sh'mai rabo," he whispered to the boy.

"Yis-kadal v' yis-kadash sh'mai rabo," the boy whispered back, effortlessly.

The old man's sons were in tears now themselves. "Rest, Poppa," one of them said, "don't tire yourself."

"I'm not tired anymore," the old man told him.

Then he wagged a finger, to summon them close. They knew the moment was at hand and lowered their heads like they did when they were children, and he blessed them.

"May God bless you and keep you. May he make his light to shine upon you, and grant you peace."

"Poppa...," one of the men said, his voice trembling.

"Amen," the old man interrupted, completing the prayer.

"Amen," the sons answered.

"You know the Kaddish?"

They shrugged. All three of them.

"Yis-kadal v' yis-kadash sh'mai rabo," the boy incanted, and made his grandfather smile.

"You will learn it," the old man commanded.

Yes, Poppa.

"You will recite it for me." Yes, Poppa.

"Every day, for eleven months." Yes, Poppa.

"And you won't forget?"

No, Poppa.

Kaddish

"Okay," the old man said, and he closed his eyes and died.

BENNY THE HEALER

It happened less than a year ago. A few witnesses thought it was a miracle, but Benny wasn't buying it.

He didn't believe in miracles. Or wonders or marvels or any other magic, but he was in fact – and saw no irony or contradiction in it – very superstitious. He was by profession a gambler – mostly horses and big league sports – and he trusted only two things, numbers and lucky charms.

But when it happened, this thing that happened, he felt it. In his belly, whatever it was that happened.

There was no mistaking it. It rocked him and he took it for a sign, so when he got home he called in and bet against all his morning wagers, zeroing everything out, just to be safe because the thing that had happened scared him.

Just after he had touched the woman, he saw a sore erupt on the back of his hand that hadn't been there before.

Like a large blister.

The woman whose shoulder he had touched was in tears. She was astonished, ecstatic. "Oh God," she whispered. "Oh my God."

She touched her breast. Gently. Then she squeezed. Pressed. So matter of fact and without any of the embarrassments that might have accompanied feeling herself up in public. "It's gone," she finally cried out, clutching Benny's arm. "It's gone."

It had been less than two months since her first diagnosis. A large tumor in her right breast. She and her family still struggled with treatment options, and there were none she wasn't shying away from. Everyone on her health care team (including the casual confidants she met at meetings and so on) urged her to action. To move forward. This was no time for patience. And while she knew that, she kept balking.

There was no way she could afford to save her life. Too late to move to another state. Her insurance coverage, which she had imagined was more than adequate – quarter of a million dollar hospital ceiling – would be completely consumed before they even got by round one.

The hospital – a Catholic generosity – said it would help with grants and discounts and so on, but preliminary calculations left her barren of hope. The house would have to go. Her grandmother's jewelry, which had been earmarked for the kids' college, would barely cover the first year of meds. Their retirement travel fund – their emergency stash – was already now fully invested in electronic wizardry and nuclear gadgets down in the basement of the hospital. There was no way she'd sacrifice her family's future for her own.

She couldn't tell them it was for money that she'd forego treatment, they'd never understand. Would never forgive her. So she told them she'd seen more people die of the treatments than the cancer and she wouldn't subject herself to that. Simply wouldn't.

She had come to the Cathedral to pray, more for guidance than miracles because she wasn't one to beseech God for personal favors. She had no trouble bending her knee for others, for friends, or strangers who might never even know, but not for herself. To pray for herself was too clearly a sin of pride, and she couldn't bring herself to do it. No, she came to the church because it was a reverently quiet place in which it might be possible to discover some peace in her own resignation.

But this one time, she prayed anyway. Not aloud. To herself – Oh God help me I'm so scared – and never even moved her lips. She prayed until her knees hurt so much she had to stand up and she left with no more clarity than when she'd arrived.

She walked across the Square in the direction of the small cafe where she'd left her family. She had wanted the time alone, and they were gracious enough to give it to her fully and wholly with no emotional envy or familial whining.

She was walking back to them when she saw the old man – Benny – standing beside a huge old oak tree, caressing a leaf with which he seemed to be completely taken. Fully absorbed in this single leaf, it felt unusually healthy to the touch. He hadn't noticed the woman and was surprised when she approached and addressed him.

"Do you need help with something?" she asked.

She was lovely, he thought, but so troubled. "Are you alright?" he answered.

"Yes," she assured him. "I just worried that you looked a little lost."

"That I am." The reason he was so enraptured with the leaf was that it had grazed his forehead as he passed by under the tree. He took it immediately for a sign. Couple of years ago a leaf blew in through his window and landed on Kobe Bryant's picture in the papers, opposite the race results.

Benny took it for a sign and bet big that night on the Lakers, and won big. He figured this new leaf must also be a sign, but he was troubled. Lakers weren't playing tonight, so it couldn't be that. There was something going on in Arizona but he never, never bet golf. Didn't trust it. Horses'll run their hearts out if you ask them to, but golfers, you just never know.

The leaf was telling him something but he just couldn't figure it.

"Where are you trying to—" the woman pursued.

"Oh no," he smiled, "not that kind of lost."

"Ah." She could most certainly empathize. "Me too."

"You're going to be fine," he told her, not sure quite why he said it, or even what he meant by it.

"Thank you," she answered, knowing that he meant well.

Everybody knew that Benny meant well. He was a happy and generous guy, a partial explanation for why he was a small time under-the-radar gambler and not one of the serious businessmen with an armed posse.

He liked people. The kids on the block adored him. Win or lose, Benny always had something for the kids. His walk home was always heralded by the neighborhood kids sounding the bells – It's Uncle Benny. It's Uncle Benny.

They loved him, and not only because he was to them a walking treasure chest. Candies. Bubble gum.

Useless souvenirs. Ice cream if the truck happened to be around. But something, always something. Flowers for his wife, every day, win or lose, when she was still alive. And all too frequently, groceries or rent money for some neighbor in trouble.

The woman understood that Benny couldn't possibly know what was wrong with her, or that even with the surgery and radiation and a loving family and think-positive exercises, the most optimistic prognosis was a couple of years, three at the most. So no, she wasn't going to be fine but there was something wonderful about Benny saying so.

"No," he said, as if he could see what she was thinking. "No, you are, you're going to be fine."

He put his hand on her shoulder and she instantly felt that something certain had altered her universe. "Oh God," she whispered. "Oh my God."

She felt faint, but wonderful. Benny caught her before she fell.

Her family saw her crumble and rushed from the cafe to the rescue. They found her weeping and feared the worst, that the doctors had told her something they'd withheld until now.

"It's gone," she cried. "It's gone."

"Of course it is," her mother agreed. "Of course it is."

"No. Feel it yourself." She was weeping now for all the days she hadn't. She took her mother's hand and held it to her breast. Guided it. "You see," she said, squealing out triumph between sobs.

"Yes, Sweetheart." Her mother cried with her. "Yes."

But hers were tears of despair. "Yes dear," if it makes it easier, then yes dear is what she'll say.

"No you don't understand. He touched my shoulder." "Yes, Sweetheart."

"No, no. Ask him. Ask him," she insisted pointing toward the tree, but Benny was gone. "The old man touched me. You must have seen him."

It surprised no one that she wished it so. And cathedrals can be overwhelming. Of course she wanted a miracle. Anyone would in her situation. Maybe everyone. Best, they all agreed without having to discuss it, to simply go along. There was no harm in letting her believe she feels better. Except of course that it might keep her away from some genuinely helpful state-of-the-art therapies.

They looked for Benny, but he was gone. Something terrible had happened and he wanted no part of it. He just wanted to get home, treat the blister, and never think about it again. Which was for him, impossible. He got old thinking about things. It was too late to stop, and this, this lucky charm business had finally shred his universe.

He'd heard someone say miracle and that scared the hell out of him. He was no friend of God, and God certainly was no friend of his.

Order is what mattered to Benny. You can't be superstitious without order. Chaos promises nothing. It didn't matter to him, God, no God, it was all the same and it explained nothing to him. But the need for it, the apparently universal preoccupation with the notion of God, that he got.

A miracle, God or not, defiled order. Stuff working like it's supposed to, that's the miracle. Planets whirling around their stars with absolute predictability. Gravity stuck tight, infallible. That the universe was reliable, that was the miracle.

So what the hell, how could he explain that blister on the back of his hand? All he knew for certain was that this day could only foment trouble for him. No good could come of it.

It wasn't as if he had called upon some higher power when he touched her shoulder. It was from the heart. He reached out just to comfort her, but the instant his fingers landed on her shoulder, he felt what she felt, that the universe had shifted. Though he never saw the flash or anything like it, it felt like lightning looking for a place to land had found his hand, which would account for the blister.

What followed were the worst six months of his now rapidly waning life. The very first sign for him was the notoriety. Word spread like a secret, some old man had made a miracle and it didn't take the neighborhood long to discover it was Benny.

Most of Benny's professional life was illegal, especially the bets he booked. He wasn't licensed, supervised, connected or otherwise protected. Most of his clients boasted a lifetime connection. They trusted Benny, and he trusted them.

He was famous in the trade for his memory. He was so paranoid about getting busted that he kept nothing on paper. Hardly ever taxing his extraordinary memory, he committed nothing to paper. Not his clients' names, phone numbers, addresses, wins, losses or balance. Box scores and so on were immediately available online so that took up no brain space, but the horse races, that's where he got his reputation.

Eight races a day from four different tracks. Win, place, show and also ran. Players had to know, just had to know, instantly, how they had done. Media was ridiculous and even the internet too slow. So Benny had confederates at each of the tracks he worked and they reported in the moment the results were posted. As they were being posted, in fact.

"Benny, me, Churchill. Fourth. Number 7 – 3.10, 2.70, 2.20. Number 2 – 18.60. 9 even. Number 5 – 4.20. Also running, 1, 3, 8, and the 6 scratched."

"Got it."

Click.

Eight times a day, four different racetracks, and he never made a mistake. And all because he was too worried to write it down on paper. You just never knew who was watching.

Notoriety was the last thing in the world that he wanted, but it played out immediately. Neighbors whispered about him. Kids began hiding from him. They all figured anyone that powerful was too dangerous to get close to. Who knows what he might do next, or where in fact his power comes from. They never see him in church and isn't that suspicious?

Strangers overcame their fear with need. They chased after him for healing or stock market tips. Blessings for their pets and even atheists searching out validation for their aspirations. It stunned him to discover how many people looked outside themselves for answers.

For a moment, because his life on the edge was always about that, seizing the moment, he considered taking advantage. He watched enough television to have studied the charlatans. "Be healed!" he heard them preach. "Send the money to me, and within three days God will grant your prayerful desires."

He'd seen the hat go 'round the virtual hall, he'd seen the address flashed on the screen where God would be accepting payment, and from where He would be dispensing miracles.

He enjoyed contemplating the mountains of cash that would arrive with each mail delivery, but that was as far as it went. He couldn't do it, it just wasn't him.

It was gradual but he found himself getting more and more cut off from the world he had formerly so fully embraced. He felt crushed by the attention, both the pleasant encounters and the besucked ones. But mostly he avoided going out because it scared him to think he might accidentally heal someone else.

As a cautionary measure, he stayed away from the Cathedral, away from the park, away from anywhere he thought anyone might recognize him.

He found himself stalking the street instead of walking it like a man would with nothing to hide – neither articles nor attitudes. He felt like a fugitive. A hit and run driver with a car freshly repainted a brand new color. A shoplifter witnessed by all but the storekeeper. An umpire who screwed up in front of 20 million enraged viewers.

One damn healing and you're screwed for life.

It was absurd, he thought, to feel this guilty just for helping someone, if in fact he had. Was this, he wondered, the much heralded punishment for committing a good deed? Or, and this he knew was the worst of it, he had upset the natural order of things. He had derailed, at the very least, his own world and this late in life, it was not a good thing to do.

The worst was yet to come. His hunches began to fail. His lucky charms ran out. Even his most trusted rituals denied him. He began a losing streak the likes of which he had never experienced before. He couldn't call a game, cover a spread, or draw a card. He felt like he couldn't even summon a red light anymore.

Fucking good deeds. He hadn't even meant it. He had lived his whole life avoiding the extraordinary, avoiding even the slightly more or less than ordinary. And healings!? Just no spot for it on the chart, no way to mark it even in his imagination, so it was clear that he was being punished, that he had set something in motion that would most certainly kill him.

Hobbled with the dread, more isolated by the day, he found himself withering away. He found himself fearing everything. He found himself a stranger, even in the mirror where nothing much had seemed to change.

Three months in he found himself watching the woman on a local morning talk show. It was Breast Week or something like that and she was on some survivors panel.

She looked great. Untroubled. Healthy. She was wearing a sweatshirt that said "Think Pink" and she was talking about her miraculous cure.

"I am absolutely cancer-free," she said with considerable humility. "The doctors can't explain it. I can't explain it, but I have to tell you I feel reborn."

Benny wondered if that's what happened, that he had traded his life for her. That whatever vital force was left in him had somehow taken refuge in her. He hated the thought, but it made sense to him.

Balance. The universe wasn't out of order, it was just shifting a little.

"I'm not saying," the woman said, "that what worked for me would work for everyone but I spent months seeking treatment and it was a losing battle."

Benny remembered the haggard look in her eyes that day at the park. He remembered everything – the lucky leaf, her kindness, the blister.

"The thing is," she said, "I know this, not ten minutes after I left the Cathedral, I was cured. Cured."

Hearing her forget about him made Benny happier than he'd been in a very long time. It liberated him. In an instant he decided it wasn't the signs and symbols or the rituals and superstitions that had gone astray.

It was him. He'd been reading them wrong.

Think Pink – it's so fucking obvious. There's a filly, big longshot running at Belmont. He called his bookie who wondered where the hell he had been and put a lot of money on her.

"You sure, Benny? She's going off at thirty, thirty-five to one."

"It's only money," Benny answered.

Even before he learned that she paid off at forty-two to one, Benny knew the spell was broken. The curse had been lifted. Benny was back.

He went out for a walk. The kids on the street were happy to see him again, waved like he'd never been gone. He stopped in at a local club for a couple of hands of poker, both of which he took, and then some lottery tickets for the hell of it.

By late afternoon he was at the cemetery with blooming new flowers for his wife. He arranged the flowers with extra care and apologized for not yet occupying the space beside her. He placed a pebble on her headstone and told her to be patient. He'd be a while yet.

— ◊ —

Morrie Ruvinsky *is an award-winning writer and filmmaker. As a writer/producer he has made a dozen movies and several television series. His acclaimed debut novel* (Dream Keeper) *was named to the Los Angeles Times Best Books of the Year.*

THE RE-ISSUE OF
DREAM KEEPER
is available from Amazon, Kindle, and other fine booksellers

"When a fishing boat pulls a naked man from the cold Pacific waters, the crew is shocked to find him still alive; even more perplexing, the large shark bite in his abdomen mysteriously heals itself. So begins this fluid, engaging first novel, which weaves together Native American folklore and mythology, pioneer history and contemporary times. The circular epic wraps up with dramatic flair and spiritual vision. This mystic, satisfying work, written with grace and authority, is rich in down-to-earth prose that moves easily and convincingly between mythic lore and contemporary dialogue."

—*Publishers Weekly*